Alison's Trumpet
and Other Stories

SHORT STORIES BY

Nat Hentoff

Jean Davies Okimoto

Phyllis Fair Cowell

Suzanne McCabe

SCHOLASTIC INC.

New York Toronto London Auckland Sydney
Mexico City New Delhi Hong Kong

COVER ILLUSTRATION BY
JOHN C. WARD

INTERIOR ILLUSTRATIONS BY
CHRIS BATISTA

"Alison's Trumpet" © 1991 by Nat Hentoff was first published in
Scholastic SCOPE® magazine, Vol. 40, No. 3, September 20, 1991.
"Watching Fran" © 1995 by Jean Davies Okimoto was first published in
Scholastic SCOPE® magazine, Vol. 44, No. 4, October 6, 1995.
"What Are Friends For?" © 1987 by Phyllis Fair Cowell was first published in
Scholastic SCOPE® magazine, Vol. 36, No. 5, October 16, 1987.
"A Difficult Call" © 1993 by Scholastic Inc. was first published in
Scholastic Action® magazine, Vol. 16, No. 12, April 2, 1993.

ISBN 0-439-05707-8

5 6 7 8 9 10   23   06 05 04 03 02

TABLE OF CONTENTS

Alison doesn't care that everyone says only guys can really play the trumpet.

ALISON'S TRUMPET

BY NAT HENTOFF

Alison was switching stations on the radio one evening when she stopped and shouted with pleasure. It was a horn, a trumpet, soaring through the air right at her. Its bright, crisp notes were singing, actually singing, a melody. But the melody kept taking on different shapes and colors, as if the horn were playing with the music.

She felt so good, she shouted again.

"What's the matter?" Alison's mother rushed into her room. "Where does it hurt?"

"Oh, it doesn't hurt. Just the opposite. Listen! Listen to the music!"

"Sounds like jazz to me," her mother said. "I never could make heads or tails out of it."

Alison's father came into the room. He listened and pointed to the radio. "That's Dizzy Gillespie," he said. "Greatest jazz trumpet player in the whole entire galaxy."

"Dad!" Alison was jumping up and down. "I've

got to have a trumpet. I've got to!"

"You have a flute," her mother said. "You're studying the flute. That's just right for a girl. Whoever heard of a girl taking up the trumpet?"

"I'm afraid your mother's right," Alison's father said. "Trumpets aren't made for girls. Or women. It takes a lot of strength to get a sound out of that horn. In the whole history of jazz, there have been no great women trumpet players. A few, a very few, women have broken in, but hardly anyone remembers their names. Stick to playing the flute, honey."

"But the flute doesn't explode in the air like firecrackers," Alison said. "The flute is like an instrument that wears dresses all the time, and you know I'm not that kind of girl."

Alison was, however, a most persistent kind of girl. She kept asking, demanding, holding her breath, for a trumpet. And she got one. Her teacher, an elderly man who used to be in the local orchestra, told Alison, "I can't teach you jazz. But you will never be able to play jazz, or anything else, until you know how to play the trumpet. And *that* I can teach you."

"Even if I'm a girl?" Alison asked.

"What has that got to do with it?" he said. "If

you want to learn, you'll learn. It's really just as simple as that."

Alison learned to play the trumpet, and two years later she applied to join the school jazz band. The director of the band, a large, gloomy man in his forties, looked at her and said, "Too young."

"Is that written down?" Alison asked. "That 13 is too young to try out?"

Another trumpet player, tall and lean, was standing behind Alison. "Nobody ever said anything about age," he said to the director, "as long as you can play."

The band director glared at him. "Girls can't play trumpet."

"Where is that?" the tall trumpet player asked. "In the Bible? In the Constitution? I must have missed it."

"Yeah," said Alison. "How can you say that until you've heard me?"

"Okay," said the director, in a tone that said it wasn't okay at all. "There's a rehearsal at two o'clock. You and you," he pointed to Alison and her new ally, "will both sit in."

As they walked away, the young man held out his hand. "Ben Stovall," he said.

Alison smiled. "I'm Alison. I wish I knew what was going to happen in that tryout," she said.

"He'll ask you to do two things," Ben told her. "First, you'll read through the music. Then he's going to ask you to improvise, to get up and take a solo based on part of the music you've just read. Can you do that?"

"Yeah. For a couple of years now, I've been putting on the radio and improvising right along with the music," Alison said. "I've even improvised along with Dizzy Gillespie. Not in person, I mean."

"You are really serious, aren't you?" Ben said.

"I'm going to be a jazz musician," Alison said. "I've been doing a lot of research lately. I bet you didn't know that there was once a great woman trumpet player."

Ben laughed. "Valaida Snow."

"And she had her own band," Alison said. "She toured Europe and the Far East."

"She had a big tone. And man! She knew how to swing!" Ben said.

"Yeah," said Alison. "I've heard the records. I bet when she was young, all kinds of people told her that trumpets weren't made for girls."

That afternoon at the rehearsal, Ben Stovall went first. He sailed through the reading part, and his improvised solos were so fresh and lyrical that the players in the band applauded. Even the band director tried to smile, but the effort was too much for him.

"Nice work," said one of the trumpet players to Ben.

Alison, who had been warming up in the dressing room, sat down in the trumpet section to take her turn. The band director called for an arrangement of Duke Ellington's "Take the 'A' Train"—a rolling, joyous piece. Playing with the section, Alison's reading was perfect.

Then the band director signaled her to take a solo. "Remember Valaida Snow!" Ben whispered to her as she stood up. Alison, remembering the first shock of jazz pleasure she had heard on the radio, felt as if she were soaring over the band, finding sounds of celebration she had never played before. Looking down, she saw Ben Stovall nodding and smiling.

"Huh?" said the trumpet player next to Ben. "She must have memorized that. No girl could make up a solo like that."

"I'll tell you what," said Ben. "You find the record that has that solo, and I will give you one hundred dollars. Okay?" The other trumpet player didn't answer. He just shook his head, fighting the knowledge that Ben was right. The solo had been Alison's—and no one else's.

The band director came over to Alison and Ben. "Rehearsal at noon on Saturday."

"We're in?" Alison asked.

"I said Saturday. At noon." The band director walked off.

"Someday," said Alison, "I'm going to come back here with my own band and ask that old walrus to sit in."

"He might surprise you." Ben smiled. "Like you surprised him today. You never know. You never know what's going to happen in this music. And whom it's going to happen to. That's what makes jazz so much fun."

"Yeah," said Alison. "And it's all just beginning for us."

Do you think Alison will make it as a jazz trumpet player?

Everyone in Zeke's family is a winner. Will Zeke ever feel that he's not a loser?

WATCHING FRAN

BY **JEAN DAVIES OKIMOTO**

"FLYING FRAN—FIRST AGAIN!" There was the headline and there was her picture, a huge one, plastered right on the front page. The *Rainier Heights Rocket* had just been delivered to our homeroom, and all across the room, newspapers rustled as everyone stared at the photo of famous Fran. "That girl is something else!" "Look at those legs!" "Is she flying, or what?"

Have I ever been mentioned in this paper? Even once, in my entire high school career—freshman, sophomore, or this year, my junior year? No, I have not. It's been three years that I've been going to this school and not once has my name ever appeared in the *Rocket*.

"Great about your sister, Ramos." Randy Woo waved the paper from across the room.

"There go Flo-Jo's records!" Sabrina Brown said.

"Maybe she'll break Jackie Joyner-Kersee's records, too," said Mary Anne Derige.

"She's going to be one of the great ones," I mumbled, smiling a lame smile.

Don't get me wrong about the lame smile. It's not that I have a problem with my sister Frances Jean's success. I'm as proud of her as anybody. Who wouldn't be?

Last year when she was only a junior she broke the all-city record in the girls' 300-meter hurdles. This year she has a shot at taking state. The track coach from the University of Oregon who recruited Fran for next year said that she's the best hurdler he's seen in his entire career. He thinks Fran can make the Olympic team.

Of course I'm proud! The only thing I don't like is when people start wondering what happened to *me*. Someone always has to ask. This time it took about three seconds.

"Did you ever go out for track, Zeke?" Mary Anne looked over at me as she thumbed through the paper.

"No," I said.

"How come?" she asked.

"I'm slow," I said.

"Oh," she said.

"I go for walks," I told her.

Mary Anne gave me a funny look. Then she opened her purse and took out a lipstick, stroking

it carefully over her mouth. "Didn't you have a brother who was great, too?"

"Yeah," I said. "Junior."

"Junior?" she asked.

"Dennis Ramos, Jr.," I said. "He's named after our Dad, but everyone calls him Junior."

"Oh, Junior Ramos. I've seen that name," she said. "It's on one of those plaques in the front hall by the trophy case, right?"

"That's right." I smile another lame smile.

Now you'd think it would be bad enough to have two track superstars in one family—with you not being one of them. But it doesn't stop there. There are six kids in our family, and every single one (except me) is outstanding at something.

Junior, the oldest, you already know about. He's our first track star.

Then there's Elaine. She's practically a concert pianist. She played with the Seattle Youth Symphony and now she goes to college at Julliard.

Ivy is next. She's a mega-brain. Ivy goes to Howard University, and she has a full scholarship.

Then there's Frances Jean, who you know about. Flying Fran Ramos, Olympic material.

Then comes me, Zeke, who doesn't do anything.

Then, last but not least, is the youngest, Jolie. She's an actress. She's been in three plays at the

Seattle Children's Theater and in two movies. They were TV movies that no one has ever heard of, but her acting coach thinks Jolie has what it takes to go all the way. That's it, folks, the Famous Ramos family . . . five stars and one dull guy.

Even our parents are outstanding, which makes sense with so many amazing kids. My dad is an engineer, and is one of the top-ranked amateur golfers on the West Coast.

Mom is a manager at an advertising agency, and this week she's back in Washington, D.C., to get an award from the Links. The Links is a service organization for outstanding African-American women. She's African American and our Dad is Filipino, which makes us a Filipino-African-American family.

Dad is out of town, too. Every year in the spring he goes to California for a big golf game, and each year he takes one of the kids with him. This year it's Jolie's turn. (They're also going to talk to some talent agents in Los Angeles when they're down there.) So it's just me and Fran at home.

"When Frances Jean goes to regionals, we're counting on you, Zeke," Mom told me as she left for the airport. "You've got to represent all of us. Remember, when you cheer for Fran, you're shouting for the whole family."

I wasn't sure if one dull guy could convey enough enthusiasm for the whole bunch of us, but I told her I'd try.

Our family is very big on support. When I was in kindergarten, Fran and Junior started calling me "Meek Zeke." Mom was furious. "We're not one of those families that is nice to strangers and nasty to each other," she yelled. "It's a fierce world, and this home is the place where we get the fuel to go out into it. Love Fuel—you can't do without it! It's as important as food! We support and encourage each other in this family and don't let me ever hear that 'Meek Zeke' garbage cross your lips again!"

After that, the only person who calls me "Meek Zeke" is me sometimes, to myself.

On Friday I left right after the last bell to drive up to Fran's meet. It was held at a college in Everett, about an hour's drive from Seattle.

I walked into the stadium and headed toward the stands. Fran was warming up, stretching in the middle of the track. I waved to her and she gave me a thumbs-up.

The stands didn't usually fill up until after five-thirty when parents got off work. I found a seat in the third row. There was only one other person down on the other end, a girl. I didn't stare, but as I walked toward the middle of the row and put my pack down, I could see that she was pretty.

I've been going to track meets ever since I can remember. By now I've gotten a bit bored with the whole thing, except when Fran runs. I pass the time reading, writing, and feeding birds. I usually carry crumbs to feed any that are around.

A flock of Canada geese flew over the stadium in perfect formation. Beautiful. It amazes me how they do that. A little sparrow hopped on the steps near me, and I threw some crumbs to it. Then I took out a notebook and decided to write about that flock of geese.

Down on the track, the boys' 300-meter hurdles started. The crowd cheered, and the girl at the end of my row was yelling, cheering, and basically going nuts. As she was jumping, the sun broke through the clouds. She looked almost gold in that light. Her hair was in these tiny little braids. It was coppery brown. Her skin was a warm honey-brown.

Then, still cheering, she leaped down the stadium steps and hugged this guy who had just won the 300-meter hurdles. He was a muscular guy, dark brown, with huge, powerful thighs. He was a good-looking dude, and he was lucky to have a girl like that.

Then I heard the announcer, "First in the boys' 300-meter hurdles, Ronnie Speed, Renton."

Ronnie Speed. Must be born to run with a name like that. From Renton. She probably went there too. Hmm, I thought, that's south of Seattle and only about 15 minutes from where I live. Then I woke up. Get real, Meek Zeke, a girl like that is only about a million miles away.

Fran's event was next. A whole group of Rainier Heights people were on their feet. I waved to them and went down to the track, to the first turn, where Fran likes the family to be.

"Go Fran! Take 'em Frances! Move those legs, girl! YOU CAN DO IT, FRANNY!" I yelled as loudly as I could.

She was something to watch, I'll tell you. Grace in motion, her front leg extended, skimming the bar, not breaking stride, her arm reaching forward. Like my sister Ivy says, "Fran runs like a deer."

"Go Fran! Go! You've got it, girl! Don't let up!" Fran was in front as she rounded the last turn. I thought I'd lose my voice, but I was yelling for the whole family so I had to make it good.

"Way to go, Flying Fran!" I cheered as she broke the finish line. Then I saw her coach pat her shoulder instead of hugging her, and I knew she had missed the record.

"First in the girls' 300-meter hurdle . . . Frances Ramos, Rainier Heights."

Fran ran over to the fence as the announcer read the results. I leaned over and hugged her.

"Way to go!" I said.

"Thanks for being here, Zeke," Fran said. "Maybe I can get under 43.05 on Sunday."

"I'll yell louder," I promised.

"You did great," she told me. "I could hear you at the first turn."

On Sunday, I drove Fran to the meet. She had to get there an hour early, so when we arrived, the stands were pretty empty. After I picked a spot in the first row, I got some bread crumbs and began sprinkling them around.

"Okay if I sit here?"

"Huh?" It was the girl from Renton. I couldn't believe it.

"If it's not okay . . . ," she said.

"Oh no . . . great! I mean, sure," I said.

"I wish I didn't have to come so early," she said, sitting down next to me. "Ronnie has to get here."

"Yeah, they have to warm up and stuff," I said.

"I saw you here yesterday, when your girlfriend won the hurdles. She's really something."

"My girlfriend?" I asked.

"Frances Ramos," she said. "Ronnie says she's expected to win State. You must be really proud."

"I am, but . . ."

She interrupted. "Ronnie's best time is 36.95. It's faster than the record for this meet, 36.96. He's hoping to break it today."

"Fran hopes to break a record, too," I said. "But she's not my girlfriend."

"She's not?"

"She's my sister. I'm Zeke Ramos."

"I'm Felicia Speed. I'm Ronnie's sister," she smiled. "Don't say it."

"Don't say what?" I asked. I was so blown away that she was Ronnie's sister I could hardly speak.

"Don't say that we don't look alike," Felicia said. "Everyone says that."

"I thought he was your boyfriend," I finally managed to say.

Felicia Speed laughed. "You thought that?"

"Yeah." I laughed too.

"Well, it's true that we don't look alike, except our eyes. They're both kind of hazel. We're mixed."

I looked at her eyes. They looked gold to me. Like cat's eyes. "Same here," I said. "We're Filipino-African-American."

"I thought you were Puerto Rican," Felicia said. "We're Jewish-Irish-African-American. On my mom's side, my grandmother is a Russian Jew and my grandfather is Irish."

"I was named for both my grandfathers," I told her. "Ezekiel for my mom's father. Manuel for my dad's father."

"Ezekiel . . . Manuel . . . Ramos," she said, listening to the sound of my whole name. "And they call you Zeke?"

"Right," I said.

"I'm named for my aunt, my dad's sister, who's named Felicia."

"My older brother, Dennis, is named for our dad. He's Dennis Jr. But everyone calls him Junior. He's a track star too."

"You don't run, do you?" she asked.

"No," I said.

"Me neither," she said.

"Actually, what I like is going for walks." Why did I say that? Now she'll think I'm weird. I reached into my backpack to get more crumbs.

"I know what you mean. Long walks, where you just look around," she said.

I grinned. "Yeah, where you don't try to be fast. Actually, everyone in my family is a star, except me. I just watch."

"My grandmother says that the spectators are the most important people," Felicia said.

"You're kidding," I said.

"Sure, think about it," Felicia said. "If enough people don't watch a TV program, it goes off the air. Or if enough people don't read a book, they stop printing it. If enough people don't come to a theater to watch a play, it closes. Baseball teams and other pro teams will leave for another city if people don't go. Most things can't exist without the spectators."

Suddenly there was a loud honking (geese, not cars) as a big flock took off from the park next to the stadium and flew in formation over our heads.

"Isn't that great?" Felicia looked up, shading her eyes with her hands. "Ever wonder how they do that?" She turned to me and I looked into her cat eyes.

"Always," I said.

The meet started, and Felicia and I talked through the whole thing. I've never enjoyed a track meet so much. She also fed the sparrows with me.

Then it was time for the hurdles. We went down to the track together and cheered like crazy.

The boys ran first. I yelled for Ronnie the way I do for Fran. Not only did he win, but with the record-breaking time of 36.93 seconds! Felicia threw her arms around me, she was so excited.

When Fran ran her race in 43 seconds flat, we

were screaming and we hugged again. It just happened, like something you couldn't stop.

That night I wrote about Felicia, about her gold cat eyes. Maybe someday I'll get the nerve to show it to her. Maybe someday next week, after the walk we're going to take. I'm leaving right after school. It's only 15 minutes to Renton.

What do Zeke and Felicia have in common? What do they have to offer that others might not?

Nancy gets a great job at a music store. Now everyone suddenly wants to be her friend.

WHAT ARE FRIENDS FOR?

BY PHYLLIS FAIR COWELL

Things were looking up for the holidays. My boyfriend Monroe found an after-school job at a discount toy store. He worked in the stock room. It wasn't a fantastic job. But it would help him buy a few presents.

I got a fantastic job. It didn't pay any more than Monroe's job. But I wasn't in a dark back room, the way he was. I worked the cash register at Rick's Music Store. Rick's did a lot of business. Just about everyone in town bought CDs and tapes there. That made me nervous at first. The crowds didn't worry me. It was all the money they handed over.

"What if someone tries to steal it?" I asked Rick, the owner.

"Why? Are you thinking about it?" he asked with a laugh.

"No!" I snapped back.

"Relax," he said. "I trust you. I checked your school references. Your grades aren't great, but

23

your teachers think you're honest. Anyway, that's not how we lose money."

He left without explaining. And there I was—in charge of the most popular place in town. Rick was usually there, but he stayed in his office most of the time.

"Hi, you're . . .?"

"Nancy," I said. "And how are you, Elaine?"

"Okay," she said, smiling at me.

For three years we had passed each other at school. She had never smiled before. Elaine was someone *other* kids smiled at. Everyone seemed to know her—or wanted to. I smiled back at her and rang up the price for two CDs. She paid and started to leave. Then she stopped and asked, "Are you coming to the party Saturday night?"

"I didn't know about it."

She wrote down the name and address of the person giving the party. "See you there," she said. "And bring a friend."

I felt really good after she left. And she wasn't the only person who began talking to me. Two guys on the basketball team came in. One of them was in my biology class. He said, "Hey, I didn't know you worked here."

"I just started," I explained.

"You're Kathy, right?"

"Nancy," I corrected him.

"Oh, yeah. See you at the next game."

I smiled as he walked off toward the records.

"Are you flirting?" a voice close to my ear asked. It was Monroe.

"Why not?" I joked. "Do you think you're my one and only?" He knew he was.

"That's what I came to find out," he said. "Actually, I got off early. I thought I'd wait and walk you home."

"That's nice," I said. "Oh, we've been invited to a party."

"Anyone I know?"

"Just one of my many friends," I laughed.

Monroe wandered around the store, waiting for it to close. Rick came out to count the money. He started to open the cash register. He stopped when he saw Monroe. "Is that guy shopping or just hanging around?" he asked.

"He's waiting for me," I said.

Rick nodded and opened the register. But he never really took his eyes off Monroe.

The next week was fun. The party was great, although Monroe didn't think so. Elaine introduced us to everyone. They were all kids from school, but we had never really met them before.

Monroe thought they were snobs.

So I went to the basketball game alone. I had a wonderful time. The guys who had invited me got me a seat in front. As I watched the game, I thought about my job. I got a good discount on CDs and tapes. Still, I would have to save more money. I had more friends to buy presents for this year.

My new friends came into Rick's often. Usually I was too busy to spend much time with them. But they always spoke to me. It was good to see them—until one cold, rainy day.

Very few people were shopping. One of the basketball players and two kids from the party came in. They said hello to me. Then they went over to the CDs. Suddenly one of the guys slipped some CDs into a pocket. At least, I thought he did. But he was so at ease about it. When he saw me watching, he waved! Maybe I didn't see right. I didn't say anything when they left. But I kept thinking about it.

"Hey, wake up." It was Elaine.

I wanted to tell her what was on my mind. But another customer came up to the cash register. And Elaine walked off. I took care of the customer. Then I saw it happen. This time I was sure. Elaine had slipped two CDs into her handbag. I hurried over to her and said, "Hey, what are you doing?"

Elaine looked around quickly and whispered, "Be quiet."

"But you put some CDs in your bag. You're not going to steal them, are you?"

"Hey, come on," Elaine said nervously. "Everyone does it."

"You could get into trouble."

"No. I won't. You're the only one who saw me." She smiled. "And anyway, what are friends for?"

Those words and that smile seemed to hang in the air. My heart was pounding. Suddenly Elaine headed for the door. Rick had appeared to help me close up.

"See you in school," Elaine said. She almost bumped into Monroe as he walked in.

"Nancy," Rick said, "let's count this money."

I walked over in a daze. I didn't say a word to Monroe, who began to flip through some CDs. Rick stared at Monroe. "Listen," he said, "I know that guy is a friend of yours, but—"

"But what?" I snapped.

"Well, friends sometimes—"

I finished the sentence. "Try to take advantage of you?"

"Yes." He tried to lighten things up a bit with a laugh.

"Real friends don't," I said.

"Look, we lose a lot of CDs and tapes here. Customers lift them."

"My friends don't!" I hissed. And I knew that was no lie.

When Monroe walked me home, I didn't say much. I was thinking about my job. I couldn't lie to Rick about those kids I had thought were my friends. I could quit. Or I could . . .

The word *friends* echoed in my head. Suddenly I turned to Monroe and asked, "What do you want for Christmas?"

"Maybe you could buy me a CD," he said. "You get a discount at Rick's."

"Money is no object," I said. "After tomorrow I won't have a lot of friends to buy presents for."

Monroe looked puzzled. "Well, don't spend too much on me. Why are you trying to be so nice?"

I smiled and said, "What are friends for?"

How was Nancy's friendship with Elaine different from her friendship with Monroe?

Rio finds out that what a sick friend needs most is a good friend.

A Difficult Call

BY **Suzanne McCabe**

My best friend, Jimmy, has AIDS. About a year ago, he started getting sick all the time. He had headaches, rashes, and colds. He hardly came to school anymore. So the doctors gave him new kinds of drugs to help make him stronger.

In the beginning, the drugs seemed to work, even though Jimmy hated taking them. "I feel like Lucy Ricardo when she was in the candy factory," he said once. "Only it's not chocolate I'm shoving into my mouth, but pills. Red ones, blue ones, green ones . . ."

Some of the drugs had bad side effects. They made Jimmy's hands and feet numb. And they churned up his stomach so much that he hardly felt like eating. The doctors said he should keep taking the drugs. But everyone seems to be running out of hope.

Before Jimmy got sick he played the saxophone. He played all the time. He'd sit on the fire escape at night, playing his heart out. People on the street always stopped to listen. Some guy in film school even made a documentary about him. But there's no more music coming from Jimmy's apartment. Now he lies in bed a lot, staring out the window.

Every day, Jimmy gets skinnier. His face and arms are pale and gray. Sometimes I hate climbing the stairs to apartment 55.

Most of the other kids have stopped coming to see Jimmy. Rob Grimes used to visit, but he couldn't take it anymore. "It's just too sad," he told me one day. Susie Kael stopped coming when her mother told her she'd pick up germs in the air. I told her everyone knows that you can't get AIDS that way, but she ignored me.

This morning I bring fresh donuts to Jimmy's mother. "Rio," she says, "you're the best friend Jimmy's ever had." I sit with Jimmy for a while, but we don't have much to say. I think about how we used to shoot hoops together after school. How we'd go to music stores downtown on Saturdays, looking for old jazz albums.

"I've got to get to school," I say finally. "Dill the Pill . . ." I stop myself, thinking about all those stupid pills Jimmy has to swallow. "I guess I shouldn't call her that."

Jimmy smiles. "That's okay. Don't worry

about it. How is old Pickle Brain, anyway?"

I haven't seen Jimmy smile in a long time. I know he wishes that he could be back in history class with us. I hold his hand for a moment. "I'll call you after school," I say.

"I . . . I," Jimmy begins softly. But he seems to change his mind about what he wants to say. "Okay, Rio. See you later."

At the door, Jimmy's mother speaks to me in a low voice. "That documentary about Jimmy is going to be on TV tonight," she says. "It would mean a lot if you were here to watch it with us."

"That's great! Of course I'll be here. Did you ask any of the other kids over?"

"Jimmy won't let me," she says. Her face is puffy from all the crying she's done lately. "He feels rejected enough. He doesn't want to risk getting hurt again."

"You can count on me," I say. I walk down the hall and almost trip over Mrs. Wu's garbage can. The smell of banana peels and coffee grounds fills my nose. It's better than the smell of sickness in Jimmy's apartment—like rotten cheese mixed with disinfectant.

Outside I run into David, the superintendent. "Nice day," he says, smiling, as he sweeps the steps.

I don't answer.

"Makes you glad to be alive."

Chill, man, I think. *Leave me alone.*

Suddenly I want everybody to leave me alone, including Jimmy.

And then it hits me. Marcy Miles. She's the girl I have a crush on. She asked me over for dinner tonight! What will I tell Jimmy's mother? I'll think of something.

Before leaving for dinner, I stand by the window and look out at the fire escape. One minute I dream about dinner with Marcy, and the next minute I dread picking up the phone.

I'll just tell Jimmy's mother the truth. After all, Marcy invited me first. And Jimmy would understand how important Marcy is to me. I rehearse my speech over and over. "You see, I'd love to come, but Marcy asked me especially . . ."

When I pick up the phone, I find myself dialing Marcy's number. "Jimmy needs me," I say. "He's the best friend I ever had."

What have Rio's experiences with Jimmy taught Rio about friendship?

DID YOU LIKE THIS BOOK?

Here are two other READ 180 Paperbacks that you might like to read.

NIGHT BIRD: A STORY OF THE SEMINOLE INDIANS

A young Native American girl must make an extremely difficult decision about her future—and that of the tribe.
BY KATHLEEN KUDLINSKI

LOVE LETTERS AND OTHER STORIES

Short stories about some serious—and not-so-serious—problems in kids' lives.
BY KATE WALKER, JANE YOLEN, HEIDI ELISABET YOLEN STEMPLE, GLORIA D. MIKLOWITZ, NORMA FOX MAZER

GLOSSARY

ally a person or country that gives support to another

churned moved roughly

convey to tell or communicate

daze the state of being stunned and unable to think clearly

documentary a movie or TV program made about real situations and people

enthusiasm great excitement

extended longer or bigger

fierce violent or dangerous

formation the way in which members of a group are arranged

fuel something that is used as a source of energy

galaxy a large group of stars and planets

hurdles small fences that an athlete jumps over in a running event

improvise to make something up on the spot

identical	exactly alike
lame	weak or unconvincing
orchestra	a group of musicians who play their instruments together
persistent	to keep trying to do something in spite of difficulties or warnings
references	statements about someone's character and abilities
skimming	gliding across a surface
soaring	flying high in the air
spectators	people who watch an event
stockier	a shorter, heavier build
trophy	a prize or award